SISTER TRICKSTERS

SISTER TRICKSTERS
Rollicking Tales of Clever Females

Retold by
Robert D. San Souci

Illustrated by
Daniel San Souci

AUGUST HOUSE
Little Folk

August House Publishers, Inc.
LITTLE ROCK

For our cousins—
Miz Mary, Miz Michele, and Miz Lisa and their Mistahs

—RSS & DSS

Published 2006 by August House LittleFolk,
P.O. Box 3223, Little Rock, Arkansas 72203
501–372–5450
http://www.augusthouse.com

Book design by Liz Lester

Manufactured in Korea
10 9 8 7 6 5 4 3 2 1 HC

LIBRARY OF CONGRESS CATALOGING-IN-PUBLICATION DATA
San Souci, Robert D.
Sister tricksters : Southern tales of clever females / retold by
Robert D. San Souci ; illustrated by Daniel San Souci.
p.   cm.
Summary: A collection of trickster tales from the
American South, featuring such female animal
characters as Molly Cottontail and Miz Goose.
ISBN-13: 9-0-87483-791-9 (hardcover : alk. paper)
ISBN-10: 0-87483-791-X (hardcover : alk. paper)
1. Tales—Southern States. 2. Tricksters. [1. Folklore—Southern States.
2. Tricksters—Folklore.]   I. San Souci, Daniel, ill. II. Title.

PZ8.1.S227Skg   2006
398.20975'0452—dc22
2006040793

The paper used in this publication meets the minimum requirements
of the American National Standards for Information Sciences—
Permanence of Paper for Printed Library Materials, ANSI.48–1984.

CONTENTS

INTRODUCTION

Trickster stories are popular the world over. The folklore of countries from America to Africa is filled with tales of sly, clever, sometimes heroic, sometimes dastardly, always resourceful fellows such as Br'er Rabbit, Anansi the Spider, Coyote, Raven, and many others.

Not as well known—but every bit the equals of (and often superior to!) their male counterparts are the females, whom we here call the "sister tricksters." These include the Spanish-American figure of Sister Fox (Hermana Zorra), who always manages to get the last laugh on her stronger—but less thoughtful—cousin, Brother Coyote (Hermano Coyote); wise and playful Borreguita (Lamb), well known in Central America and Mexico; deceptive foxes or cats who assume human form in Japan, China, and many other Asian countries; and Molly Cottontail from the southern United States.

I first came across Molly in a collection of tales gathered by Anne Virginia Culbertson in the antebellum South and printed in the turn-of-the-century collection *At the Big House*. The stories, told by "Aunt Nancy" and "Aunt 'Phrony" (literary constructs who are themselves the first cousins of "Uncle Remus") tell the adventures and antics of largely female "animal folks." I retold one tale in my own *Cut from the Same Cloth: American Women of Myth, Legend, and Tall Tale*. Now there is the chance to share many more of these sister stories that were once told in *At the Big House*.

Foremost among these characters are such females of the species as Molly, Miz Grasshopper, Miz Duck, and Miz Goose. They emerge triumphant in what are sometimes life-or-death encounters with such formidable (but ultimately less "trickish") opponents as Mistah Slickry Sly-fox, Rooster, and Mistah Bear.

Even when their enemies try to play the "trickster" game themselves, "sisters" are able to see through the plotting and turn the tables to their advantage.

As "Aunt Nancy" comments in *At the Big House,* "Let me tell you that when a woman start out to be trickish she can beat a man every time, 'cause her mind works a heap faster. She see all 'round and over and underneath and on both sides of a thing. . . . Meanwhile, a man's just trying to stare plumb through it."

Tricksters by-and-large appear to hold the position of underdog in these tales. Often these tales were told by oppressed people as a way of laughing at their superiors and reassuring themselves that the meek of the earth can, at the very least, get the last laugh. This aspect—the trickster as hero of the oppressed—is nowhere seen as clearly as in the stories of John or Old John (also known as High John the Conqueror, Big John, Jack, or other common slave names) from the pre-Civil War South. He is the clever slave who matches wits with Old Massa, the plantation owner, and generally wins—but always draws a laugh even when he loses.

Many of John's tricks are the same sort used by Br'er Rabbit. They are very similar characters in many ways—no doubt drawing off the same West African traditions of culture heroes such as rabbit trickster or clever tortoise or Anansi the Spider (also known as "Aunt Nancy"—especially in South Carolina—one of the fictional storytellers in *At the Big House*). Each of these figures is by turn comic, cunning, and outrageous.

The John stories most often concern the ways a slave overcomes the restrictions of plantation life, avoids punishment, gains rewards, and even sometimes wins freedom. "In the best of the John stories," comments folklorist B.A. Botkin, "John and Massa stand in much the same relation to each other as Br'er Rabbit and Br'er Fox, each serving as a foil for the other's cunning."[1]

The tales often have a slapstick element—and even the knockabout mayhem and cruelty that characterize a Punch-and-Judy puppet show or a cartoon. But

---

[1]Botkin, B.A. "John or Old John." Article in *Funk & Wagnall's Standard Dictionary of Folklore, Mythology, and Legend,* Maria Leach, ed. New York: Harper & Row, Publishers, 1949, 1950, 1972. Paperback edition published in 1984.

the truth is that they are cautionary stories, with undercurrents of harsh wisdom (act in a rash, unthinking way, and watch out!) and reassurance (even the weakest creature can, with application of brainpower, find her or his way out of a seemingly hopeless situation).

To be sure, Molly and her cohorts often act in "scandalous" ways that have the listener or reader shaking her or his head, even as they laugh at the mischief that has been stirred up or the trick that has been played.

Author Anne Marie Kraus puts matters in perspective when she writes, "Because a trickster often behaves badly, these tales, while primarily entertaining, also communicate lessons about moral values in society. By laughing at a trickster, we recognize common human foibles and remind ourselves in a humorous way that this is not acceptable behavior. In *African Folktales,* Roger Abrahams states, 'Trickster is the figure who most fully illustrates how not to act within society . . . His antics represent just what sane and mature people do not do.' Some Coyote tales were used by native Americans to show children the path to acceptable behavior. Yet Julius Lester, reteller of Br'er Rabbit tales, observes that 'Trickster tales are not moral. . . . The reward for [Trickster's] trickery is not punishment, but, generally, victory.' Virginia Hamilton, in her collection *A Ring of Tricksters,* believes that 'the animal tricksters were invented by the community to cast away acts of human misbehavior from more suitable deeds. These animal characters . . . performed outlandish tricks because the people needed them to. We're glad they did. . . . They seem very human, very much like ourselves.' "[2]

Nearly a century ago, in the final paragraph of her *At the Big House,* Anne Virginia Culbertson noted ruefully that "Molly Hare herself has vanished"— her stories no longer being told. It is our hope that these retellings of some of the tales will bring them back into currency with a new generation of listeners and readers.

[2]Anne Marie Kraus, *Folktale Themes and Activities for Children, Volume 2.* Englewood, Colorado: Teacher Ideas Press/A Division of Libraries Unlimited, Inc., 1999.

Mistah Fox's Funeral

IN THE OLD DAYS, THERE WERE ANIMALS THAT WERE ALWAYS falling out with one another, and trying to get ahead of each other, and setting all sorts of traps and playing all kinds of tricks. Two of these creatures were Miz Molly Cottontail—who was sometimes called old Molly Hare—and Mistah Slickry Sly-fox. Sometimes one was in the lead, sometimes the other, but generally Miz Molly came out ahead, for that seems to be the special gift of the ladies, to get their own way with their brains instead of their fists. Compared to these quick-wits, menfolk often seemed kind of clumsy and lumbersome about things that needed more thinking than thumping. More times than not, they gave themselves away before they got halfway through a plan.

There was a time Molly and Slickry crossed wits with each other so fiercely that it ended with a funeral. Things seesawed so—first this one up, then down; then the other up, down—that, for a time, it was hard to guess who was going to come out on top. But, by the end of their battle of the brains, old Molly proved she was a "hare smarter" than Mistah Fox. It happened this way . . .

One day Mistah Fox came across Molly when she was good and tired, sitting in the broom-sedge field, down by the old sawmill. With a growl, he began to chase her through the woods and into the swamp and out into the field on the other side, till she was all worn down and out of breath. "Oh, me! Oh, my!" she said to herself. "I reckon this here's where I've got to turn up my little toes and give up the ghost, sure enough, 'cause I can't run another step, and it's no use to try."

Just then, as luck had it, she heard a great blowing of horns and a lot of hounds giving cry a far ways off, and she knew that the foxhunters were somewhere around, so she gathered herself together and set out in that direction. But first she made a show of waving to Mistah Fox and yelling, "You're slower than an old turtle, I declare." Then away she went, making a big show of moving pretty winded-like.

Fox couldn't resist the bait of her name-calling and the fact that she seemed so tuckered out. "I'll turtle you, Missus!" he shouted. But Molly led old Fox right into the midst of the dogs and the horses and the hunters, and then she doubled back and got out of the way in short order. Well, Mistah Slickry Sly had a mighty close shave that time—getting away with a few bites and bruises—but he never forgave Miz Molly. He declared to everyone that he was going to get even with her if he didn't do another lick that winter.

He sat by the fire and studied and studied about revenging himself on Miz Molly, with his head on his hand and his jaw dropped open, till he got sort of run down and his appetite gave out. Miz Fox was worried about him; but at the same time, she was put out with him for sitting on his haunches doing nothing and letting her scrounge around for something to eat.

One day, at last, his wife took the broom, shook it at him, and yelled, "Get out of my sight, you miserable, shiftless creature. If you go and stir yourself around and work a little, it might start your blood going and cure you, for you've got a bone disease, which they call lazy-bones, and I'm gonna cure you right here and now. I don't want no funeral around this house, with all the shrouds and the coffins and the flowers and the hearses, and the vittles for the mourners to gobble down at the wake. That'd cost me more than you've ever been worth, sir!" And with that she brought the broom *ker-smack!* down on Mistah Sly-fox's head.

That thump shook loose some real thinking in Mistah Fox's head. When he heard the word *funeral,* that gave him an idea. He sprawled there without moving, like he was sure-enough dead, and he let his wife pick him up and put him on the bed. He lay there all the while listening to her go on, wringing her hands and crying, "Oh, Heavens! Oh, Heavens! What a wicked woman I am! I killed my poor sick husband! What am I gonna do? Oh, mercy me, what *am* I gonna do?"

Fox was mightily tickled, so he let her run on awhile. He said to himself, *This here's where I find out how the old woman is gonna behave herself when she's a widow.* Moaning, he turned on his side. Then he opened his eyes like he was dreadfully feeble and rolled them up in his head, and said, "Old woman, I forgive you for this, indeed I do. But I can't expect to last much longer. Let me ask you, before I go, to give me a decent funeral, with all the fixings; and I want a sermon preached for me, too, saying how wonderful I've always been to you and to everyone. And I want you to invite all the neighbors to my wake, even Miz Molly Cottontail, 'cause I forgive her, too. You must send her word that I am gonna rest more peaceably in my grave if she'll come to the wake. And I want you to have plenty of vittles for the mourners, 'cause I don't want no person to go away from *my* funeral and say he's hungry."

Miz Fox started crying and wringing her hands again, but she gave her promise. She said, "Old man, you can die easy, for I'm gonna give you the word of a poor widow woman that you are gonna have everything that belongs with a first-class funeral—all the trimmings and the fixings thrown in, if I have to work my fingers to the bone over the washtub to pay for them. Don't you let that worry keep you lingering on in torment; I've given you my word, and that oughtta be enough to let you down into the grave on flowery beds of ease, indeed it should."

Fox thanked her, and then he gave a big groan and rolled over on his back and turned his toes up in the air and lay there as stiff as if the breath of life had gone clean out of him. He was so pleased with himself at how he'd fooled his missus that he had to make a real effort to keep a grin off his face. Pretty soon his jaw was sore from holding down a smile. And it wasn't long before all the bones in his back and arms and legs took to aching from lying so stiff-like. But he was bound and determined to pull off this trick and snare Miz Molly, so he just kept still and let his bones keep aching. Meanwhile, Miz Fox wiped her eyes on her sleeve and rushed around to get everything ready for the wake. She killed a chicken and boiled a ham and cooked a mess of greens, and then she sent word to the neighbors to come to the wake. Next she cleaned the house. Last of all she gave her attention to the corpse; and when she got through with Mistah Fox, he certainly looked more handsome than he did when he was walking through this vale of tears. She sent off for the coffin and the flowers, and when the mourners got there for the wake, everything was good and ready.

Well, she gave them a good bit of food, and they sat up all through the night moaning and groaning and droning. Every once in a while the widow would throw her apron over her head and burst into tears and rock back and forth and carry on till some of the menfolks would come and console her, and then she'd pull herself together a little. Slickry kept one eye open a bit and one ear cocked, so he caught her whispering with Mistah Coon a little and looking at him mighty sweet when she saw the rest weren't looking.

Uh-huh! he said to himself. *That's how the wind blows! It isn't many husbands who get to see what kind of widow they are gonna leave behind. Running on with old Coon right before my face and eyes! Well, if I don't pay her off for that, my name isn't Slickry Sly-fox. Widow indeed! Not for long, if she has the say-so.* And it was all he could do not to get up right then and there and pick a quarrel with her.

All through the night the mourners kept it up, rocking back and forth and singing like this—*m-um-ah-um-m, m-um-ah-um-m*—and wailing. Though now and then they'd stop for a little set-to with the food. When the morning came, all of them went home to dress for the funeral. Long about noon, here they came again, gussied up in all the fine things they could lay their hands on. Old Miz Bear was the fanciest; she had on a pink silk dress, low neck and short sleeves, with a trail and a pink sunshade to match. But Miz Panther came close, because she had on a white gown with flounces from top to bottom and bows of red ribbon with streamers behind. The gentlemen had on neckties and white cotton gloves and red handkerchiefs sticking out of their pockets. They all came in and they talked a little with Miz Fox, and she told them she was proud to see them there. After this she invited everybody to sit down.

Then someone remarked, "I declare, Sis' Molly Cottontail hasn't come yet. I wonder what makes her so late? Did any of you-all see her on the way here? I reckon she stopped to primp herself up." No one had seen her, so someone said they'd best sing a tune while they were waiting. With that they struck into "Zion Weep a-Low," with the ladies carrying the tune and the menfolks doing the humming.

Well, they finished that spiritual, and Miz Molly still hadn't come, so they said some prayers for a while. When Miz Molly still didn't show, the preacher decided it was time to begin anyway. So he got up and cleared his throat a time or two and commenced talking about Mistah Fox. He said, "Sinner friends, I want to call your attention to this corpse; you can see for yourself what a nice corpse it is, wearing real white gloves with flowers strewn all up and down him. I want you all to take particular notice of that, for that's gonna teach you how it pays to be honest and industrious. If he hadn't been that-a-way he wouldn't have such a funeral as this is, with me here, too, into the bargain, to give him a send-off, all nice and proper. And since Sis' Fox, the wife of the deceased, is going to pay me for it on time, I won't keep her waiting for the funeral sermon till next year, no sir."

Some of the mourners fetched a groan, and some of the brethren and sisters responded from the corners, "Amen! Honest and industrious, that's the truth!" Miz Fox began to squeal and fell back in her chair, and the funeral had to stop till they could bring her to with a gourd of water.

Just then, who should put her head in the door but Miz Molly Hare. But she was too smart and knew Mistah Slickry Sly too well to come close to the coffin. She was all dressed up in black, with a big bonnet, and a mourning veil more than a yard long streaming down her back, and she was carrying a big white handkerchief with a black border and a bouquet of flowers.

She greeted the others and stood a little ways off and looked at the corpse, with her head on one side and her mouth drawn down like she was mightily affected by all this. Finally she said, mopping her eyes now and then with the handkerchief, "Poor Mistah Fox, poor old Slickry! I certainly never expected to see him like this. I forgive him all the hard feelings that have passed between us. He certainly is a nice corpse, Sis' Fox, and one that you are gonna be proud of all the rest of your days. I have only one fault to find with him, and that is, his paws aren't crossed; I always heard my granny say—and she was mighty knowing—that the paws of a corpse must always be folded. He won't look like a sure-enough corpse until his paws are crossed."

At that old Mistah Slickry took and slipped one paw across the other and lay there looking as innocent as a lamb, but that was enough for Miz Molly. She knew then that it was just as she suspected all along: that Slickry was never more alive in his life.

Still sounding sad and looking teary-eyed, she said, "Just let me set these flowers alongside the corpse's head to show my feelings for him." Mistah Fox tensed up, ready to grab Miz Molly as soon as she came near the coffin. But to the startlement of the other mourners, Miz Molly flung the bouquet of flowers, which she had sprinkled with pepper, into Mistah Fox's face.

"Ker-choo!" Mistah Fox sneezed, sitting up in his coffin and rubbing his pepper-stung eyes.

"Hallelujah!" cried Molly. "It's a miracle! Mistah Fox has come back to life like Lazarus."

"Amen!" cried the old folks from the corners.

But Molly didn't waste any time. She ran off with her mourning veil streaming out behind her in the wind. Fox jumped up and knocked down the preacher and spilled all the flowers and took after her fast as he could, but he was held back by the fancy suit. Besides, he was sort of stiff and weak from lying still so long with nothing to eat into the bargain, so he didn't see more than the end of her veil whipping around a corner.

That funeral caused a lot of trouble in the Fox family. From then on, Mistah Fox would grumble to his old woman every now and then that she had carried on with Mistah Coon right in front of the corpse of her own husband. But she knew how to shut him up; she just said, "Wasn't no corpse! Though it oughtta have been, seeing all the grief it caused me. No respectable corpse would act in such a low-down way: a mannerly corpse would have known what was expected of it and *stayed* dead. And all of those mourners did all that weeping and wailing and eating up all the food at the wake. I tell you, when your time sure enough comes, I won't be able to find mourners enough in this here county to bury you decently. Folks don't like to have their feelings disappointed that-a-way! Don't you talk to me as long as we still owe money on that funeral!"

In the end, Mistah Fox learned to keep his mouth clamped as tight as when he'd pretended to be a corpse. He continued to blame Molly for his new troubles. Mostly, though, he didn't want to admit that she was smarter than him. Seems that some folks don't want to hear the truth, whether it's whispered to them or preached to them or hits them upside the head.

17

Mistah Fox and Molly Hare Go Fishing

AFTER MIZ MOLLY TURNED THE TABLES ON MISTAH Fox at the funeral, he kept on studying and scheming to get even with her. Folks who met up with him in the woods knew he was up to something, because he'd go trotting by, not stopping long enough to answer howdy. And he looked so knowing out of those slanted-up eyes of his, with his face all drawn up into wrinkles, that they could see he was planning out some sort of mischief, and they took good care to keep out of the way. Even when he was fooling the dogs—sitting up on an old log with his tongue hanging out, just as still as if he were dead, so they'd pass him by—he was studying, studying about Miz Molly. It was the same when he went down to the orchard to get a chicken, even though it's mighty hard work to get chickens that have flown to the trees.

On a cloudy night he went along underneath the tree where the fowls were roosting and found them all fast asleep. Now Mistah Fox knew that wouldn't do, because chickens lock their claws tight around the limb when they go to sleep, and their claws stay tight until they wake up. He knew he had to rouse them before he could get one. So he gave a sharp bark and jumped up, and when they started to cackle, he commenced to circle round and round underneath the tree, faster and faster, jumping and barking.

The chickens turned and twisted their necks to watch him. At last some fool fowl who was kind of weak in her head got so dizzy that she just dropped right down and he gobbled her up in a jiffy.

This goes to show that Fox is a great schemer. He never does anything in a hurry; he just plans it all out good and then takes his time to carry it off. So when he vowed he was going to get even with Molly Hare if it took him till Christmas, he was as good as his word. In fact, it was getting along toward that time before he was ready for her.

One cool morning he went streaking through the woods, lifting up one paw and stopping to listen for the dogs now and then; but the coast was clear, and he kept on till he got to Miz Molly's. He knocked on the door, but she didn't hear him because she was busy rocking Bunny and Honey, two of her children who were sick. All the while she was singing at the top of her voice to drown the noise the other children were making as they racketed around the house, playing horsey and leapfrog and tag and roughhousing and tussling. The commotion was so bad that Old Man Hare was obliged to go and sit on the bench outside the back door to get some peace and quiet.

Miz Hare kept on singing at the top of her voice:

> *Oh Bunny is my baby,*
> > *Bunny is my lamb,*
> *I love my Bunny better*
> > *Than a great big dish of ham.*

> *Oh Honey is my baby,*
> > *Honey is my lamb,*
> *I love my Honey better*
> > *Than a great big roasted yam.*

Drat this here Bunny and Honey, said Fox to himself. *Womenfolks certainly do make fools of themselves over their children, and make the children fools in the bargain.* With that he gave a big, loud knock on the door with his walking stick, and Miz Molly let out a scream and jumped so that she almost dropped Bunny and Honey. She asked her visitor to come in, and she certainly was surprised when she saw who it was; but she didn't let on, not her—that wasn't her way. She put on her best manners and asked Mr. Fox to get a chair for himself, because he could see that her hands were full. Then she began to chatter on about the weather the way folks always do when they don't know what else to say.

Fox was mighty polite and mannerly and chock-full of pretty talk. "I declare to goodness, Miz Molly Cottontail, you certainly do look sumptuous," he said. "It appears that you get younger and younger every year, you certainly do, ma'am."

Molly simpered, but she wasn't taken in by him. "Hush, man!" she said. "Better not let Miz Fox hear you go on that-a-way! Besides, I know I'm no more to look at these days than a lean crow with a graveyard cough."

"Shoot, Miz Molly," Fox said, "you aren't doing yourself justice, indeed you aren't. I never have seen you looking better. I'll back you against all the silly young gals around these parts." He ran on that-a-way until he thought he had gotten her good and pleased, and then he said, "Miz Hare, I came around to see if you would like to go fishing. I know a monstrous fine place, where the fishes are thicker than blackberries in a patch, and I'll take you right there if you say so. It's not far, either."

Miz Hare said, "Thanky, Mistah Slickry; thanky, sir. I wish to gracious I *could* go with you, but you see how it is. Here are Bunny and Honey sick on my hands—real croupyfied, they are. And the other children are cutting up like the dickens, and all my work is laying around undone. I declare that those children are gonna run me distracted. You, Blinker! You, Winker! Come here, both of you, and set yourselves down by the chimney and stop that everlasting scuffling. Jumper and Thumper, I want you to come here and shake paws with Mistah Slickry Sly-fox and act like you had some proper raising, instead of going on with that fist-and-skull-fight right in front of the company."

The children did what she told them, and Fox kept on persuading and persuading. Miz Molly was mighty fond of enjoying herself, and she wasn't too fond of housework, so at last she said, "Well, Mistah Sly-fox, I don't know how in the world I can go with you, indeed I don't. But maybe I can get the old man to look after the children. And if I leave plenty of pollygollic and squilts and horehound-and-boneset tea for Bunny and Honey, I reckon they'll get on just fine, and I can set out a cold snack for the rest of them till I get back."

So she called the old man to come in and mind the children, and he came pretty slowly, dragging his feet and looking mighty unhappy. She showed him the food and gave him the tea to dose Bunny and Honey with every time they cried. At this, the children all set up a terrible squall; but she didn't pay any attention. "Hush, now!" she said. "I'm gonna fetch a mess of fish for your supper." Then she threw on her shawl, took an old basket, and set out for the creek with Slickry Sly-fox.

On the way she said, "Mercy me, Mistah Slickry, what are we gonna do for poles and lines? I was so bothered up getting away from my children that I didn't think anything about such things."

"Never mind," the Fox said. "I took care of that. I can't be pestered carrying poles and lines back and forth, so I keep them hidden away in an old hollow tree near the creek. I'll fit you out all right, Miz Molly; don't you disturb yourself about that."

They went along mighty friendly and getting on famously, and old Fox got so monstrously polite that at last he said, "I declare to gracious, Miz Molly, you must excuse me for being so unmannerly as to let you carry that basket. It isn't proper for a lady like you to do that. Please, ma'am, let me tote the basket."

Miz Molly answered him just as nicely, saying, "Indeed, Mistah Fox, I couldn't even think of letting a gentleman like you be seen toting a basket; you mustn't mention it anymore."

Fox insisted and insisted, and Molly kept on saying she didn't want him to carry the basket, but at last she handed it over to him. (Though if there'd been anything in it, Miz Molly would never have let him tote it; she knew him too well for that.)

When they came to the creek, Fox put the basket on the ground and sat down on a log to catch his breath before he got to work. Miz Molly was eager to begin fishing, so she said that if he'd just tell her where the poles and lines were hidden, she'd go and fetch them and get the bait ready.

Fox said, "Do so, Miz Molly; do so. Just go up the stream yonder a little ways and look in that old hollow sycamore there and you'll find a lot of poles and tackle. You can go ahead and take your choice."

She skedaddled up the bank and poked her head into the sycamore tree, looking for the poles. To her surprise, there weren't any there! She was so busy thinking of catching fish that she didn't notice Mistah Fox grinning because he knew there never were any poles. She thought maybe she'd gone to the wrong tree, so she went traipsing around to every sycamore she saw on the bank and got herself all frazzled out without finding a single pole or line.

All the while, old Fox sat up on the log laughing to himself over Miz Molly and the poles. But Miz Molly was so caught by the idea of catching fish that she didn't catch on to Mistah Fox's trickishness. At last she came back and told him there wasn't any sycamore with poles inside. He said, "What's that, Miz Molly? You tell me you can't find those poles? I'm obliged to see that with my own eyes, for I can't believe it!" With that, he climbed to his feet and moseyed to the sycamore. When he got there he poked his head inside and then pulled it out and squatted down on his haunches and dropped his jaw open like he was so surprised he couldn't talk.

After a long time he said, "Well, *Miz Molly!* I'm so flabbergasted, I scarcely can get my breath. Only yesterday I was here, and those poles were all safe and sound, and now some no-count, consumbunkshus thief-of-the-world has been here and helped himself to my property. I wish I had him here this minute. I declare to you I'd just naturally wear them poles out on his hide, that I would. You'd think a halfway decent person would have left just one pole to let me still do a little bit of fishing. I've never known anyone that mean before, unless it was the man who shaved himself just before he died, so as to cheat the barber out of the job."

Then he hung his head and said sadly, "And you, Miz Molly, came all this way to go fishing, and there's no pole or tackle for you. It certainly is a shame. I just feel *terrible* for you."

Miz Molly felt kind of sorry for him, so she said, "Oh, never mind, Mistah Slickry Sly. I don't mind that so much, but I am sort of disappointed not to take home some fish to the children and my old man, 'cause I know they are all hoping for a nice fish dinner this evening."

Fox made a show of giving the matter great thought for a while, and then he said, "Well, I tell you, Miz Hare, if you are willing to fish like I sometimes do, maybe we can get a mess of fish for your family yet. Now you sit up here on the bank a minute and I'll show you that if you just have the gumption, you can get fish without any tackle. It's that-a-way in the fishing business, anyhow: you can have all the poles and lines you want, but if you haven't got the gumption, you won't get the fish."

With that he marched himself down the bank and stood on the edge of the stream with his nose near the water, peering in. Soon, along came a fool young fish that didn't know enough to realize who was staring down at her. Old Fox didn't move a muscle until the fish was right beneath his snout. Then he plunged one paw in, swiped the fish out, and landed her in the basket before she could flop her fins twice.

He called Miz Molly down to see, and she was tickled to death with the way he caught that fish. She said, "Well, I never saw the likes of that since I was born! Mistah Sly-fox, I'd be mighty grateful if you'd teach me that new-fangled way of fishing; it sure beats the old way."

Fox said, "There's no trick to doing that. All you've got to do is to put your nose down in the water and keep just as still as that rock yonder, and the first fish you see beneath your nose, just swipe your paw in and get her."

Miz Molly did like he told her and dropped to all fours there with her nose poked down so that it touched the water. She knelt there and she knelt there, but no fish came along, because old Slickry kept up a loud talking and made all the racket he could to scare the fishes away.

Still Miz Molly crouched there and she crouched there, and it got on toward night and turned colder and colder, it being December. Finally, she got tired and said she believed that she was about ready to get up and go home. But Fox egged her on and told her not to budge, because he felt sure that when the fishes came out to get their supper, they were bound to come that way. Now the water got colder and colder all the time, and Miz Molly began to shake, and her teeth chattered like she had the chilblains. At last she said, "Indeed, Mistah Sly-fox, I can't stand this any longer; indeed I can't. I have to quit this minute or drop here in my tracks; yes, I must."

Fox chuckled to himself like he knew something mighty funny. "Come along, then, Miz Molly," he said, "it *is* almost night. I reckon your children and your old man were expecting you long before this." With that he picked up the basket with the fish in it and scrambled up the bank. Miz Molly was going to follow, but when she went to lift her head, she found that her nose was frozen fast to the water, because the ice had been forming all the time she was kneeling there, and old Fox knew that very well when he called down to her from the bank. She pulled and she hauled, and she kicked and she thrashed, but it wasn't any use; there she was and there she stayed.

Fox stood high up the bank just laughing and carrying on. He got so full of laughter and fun that at last he took to chasing his own tail around and around in a circle, just the way a puppy does. Miz Molly heard him going on, and she called out, "That's all right! You got me fair and square for once in your life. High time you did, seeing how many times I fooled you. But I tell you that you're gonna laugh on the wrong side of your mouth before I get through with you, sure as my name's Molly Hare; that you will!"

She kept on twisting and turning and trying to work her nose free, but it was a long time before she got it loose, and even then she had to leave a piece of the skin sticking to the ice. When Fox saw she was free, he stopped chasing his tail around and picked up the basket and lit out into the woods without stopping to say fare-you-well. And it was a long time before he had the nerve to come anywhere near where Miz Molly was after tricking her so.

"Um-umph!" she said as she went along home. "This serves me right for being such a fool about fishing. Fishermen haven't got any sense, anyway. Seems to me that the chance of getting one of those little scaly-backed creatures just crowds everything else clean out of their heads. Look at me: no fish, nose all skinned up, a three-mile walk before me, and a hungry old man and cross children at the end of it. After this I'm gonna stay home and do the eating and let someone else do the catching."

For days her nose was aching her so that she couldn't hold it still. She kept twitching and working it to get some ease, but it seems like she never got clean over that experience, because hares have been twitching their noses ever since. Sometimes it looks like they're making faces at you and acting sort of scornful, but it isn't so; it's just because old Miz Hare got her nose frozen that time she went fishing with Slickry Sly-fox. What happened reminded Miz Molly—and all her kin—that they'd better keep their wits about them at all times. There are many different kinds of bait a trickish creature can use to hook someone, whether he's got a fishing pole or not.

The Toad,
the Grasshopper,
and the Rooster

BACK IN THE OLD TIMES, THERE WEREN'T ANY MORE lively creatures than the Toad, the Grasshopper, and the Rooster. Miz Grasshopper, who was sometimes called "Miz Pop-eyes" because of her bulgy eyes, was a great dancer; she'd twirl and jump and flounce around in the grass all day long. Some folks spoke unkindly about her silly ways.

Toad spent all his time hunting bugs and such, and the way he got over the ground was a caution to snakes that tried to make a dinner of him. He didn't stop to walk, he just naturally leaped from one place—*ker-swish!* through the air—and lit on the next place. Oh! He was a supple creature, that he was. But he had never done a minute's worth of honest work his whole life long.

Rooster was a monstrous fine performer with his voice; he didn't do much but practice his wake-up call. He was so proud of this, he wouldn't wait for dawn but got up early in the morning and woke the other folks long before daybreak, singing:

Cock-a-doodle-deedle-doo,
I can sing much louder than you,
Cock-a-deedle-doodle-dee,
Get up and listen, folks, to me!

Well, his neighbors didn't like him any too well, because he always commenced his singing just about the time when they wanted to turn over and have another little snooze. Besides that, they thought he was kind of an old hypocrite, because he strolled along with Miz Hen and the children, pretending like he was helping to scratch out a living, and the only thing he did was rush in when Miz Hen began a-cackling to announce she found a bug or a worm. Then Rooster snatched it away from her before she could say Jack Robinson.

After a while these three got the other creatures down on them, because of all their singing and dancing and shiftless ways. When they saw how unpopular they had become, they thought maybe it was time to turn over a new leaf and earn a proper living. So they got together and had a long talk and made up their minds that they were going to run a farm together. Rooster was appointed the plow hand because he had such strong claws—just perfect for scratching up the ground; Toad was to be the hoe-hand; and Miz Grasshopper was to stay home and do the cooking and look after the house.

They divided the work this-a-way for a long time, and they got on mighty well and were mighty pleased, because the newness hadn't rubbed off. But presently Miz Grasshopper got kind of tired and lazy, because, truth be told, she hadn't ever done a lick of work before in all her born days. She threw down the skillet and sat back in a chair and put her feet on a stool and tied her head up in a handkerchief and said she was feeling so "ailified" that she knew she was in for a spell of sickness. But she wouldn't let Rooster and Toad send for the doctor.

"I'm sure I'm gonna die, anyhow," she told her friends, "and I want to take my own time expiring and not be hurried into the next world by all the stuff a doctor makes folks swallow. I might as well die easy," she said, looking all teary-eyed and saying how weak she felt. But she found strength enough to talk about the doctor in a scandalous way, because she didn't want him to come there and let out the news that the only thing that ailed her was laziness.

Then she climbed into bed and lay there groaning and carrying on. The menfolks stood around and looked at her awhile, sort of helpless, and then they said, "Well, I reckon there isn't anything we can do." So they went off to work. Since Rooster was plowing in a far field and Toad was hoeing near the house, they agreed that Toad had better get dinner. So he had to do the hoeing and the cooking and tidying up the house. He was also waiting on Miz Grasshopper; she found something for him to do every five minutes during the day.

They kept it up that-a-way until Toad was worn to a frazzle, and he decided he had to have something or other to cheer him up and drive his weariness away. About that time he came across the rim of an old meal-sifter and that put an idea in his mind. He took the frame and stretched a piece of sheepskin over it, and then he got a piece of fence-rail and whittled it down and fastened it on the rim. Presently he found an old cow-horn and he carved that into pegs. Then he got some catgut strings and stretched them across the sifter. He screwed them up with the cow-horn pegs until he got them in tune. Lastly, he swiped one hand across the strings and *presto!* The strings gave a musical strum, and he had a sure-enough banjo—one of those regular old plinketty-plunketty banjos that have more git-up-and-go to them, when it comes to making hands clap or feet dance, than any of the shiny, primped-up banjos that hang in a store window and try to get folks to walk in and buy them.

When Mistah Toad got his banjo all tuned up, he sat outside the door every day while dinner was cooking and played tunes that would make even folks who never danced a step in their lives feel like they just had to get up and tap their feet. One day while he was picking out a lively tune, Toad was sure he heard the sound of dancing on the floor inside. "Day of grace!" he cried. "Are my ears fooling me, or is that dancing? Can't be Miz Grasshopper, 'cause she's too poorly. It *must be,* though, since she is the only person in there."

He stopped playing, the dancing stopped; he played again, the dancing went

31

on. He put his ear against the banjo belly, shook it, and listened to see if anything rattled. But the banjo was working all right, so then he *knew* it was Miz Grasshopper. He didn't let on, and he waited on her just the same. But when Rooster came home, Toad took him off a little ways. "Mistah Rooster," he said, "when you come back to dinner tomorrow, don't get up on the fence and crow like you've been doing to let me know it's time to dish up the dinner; instead, while I pick my banjo, you creep up softly and peek in through the door."

"Well," the Rooster asked, "what's in the wind now, Mistah Toad?"

"Never mind," said the Toad. "You go on and do like I tell you, and I promise you'll see a sight for sore eyes."

So when Rooster came home to dinner the next evening, instead of crowing to say he'd be there soon, he crept up to the door and peeked in through the crack while Toad picked the banjo so tunefully it seemed the rocks and the trees would have to step in time. And beyond the door there was Miz Grasshopper, dancing around the room just as well as she ever had. She capered and she twisted and she turned. She did fancy dance steps like the back-step and the pigeonwing and wound up with the double shuffle. Last of all she leaped up and clacked her heels together and spun clean around in the air before she lit on her feet.

Rooster didn't say anything; he just beckoned Toad. Toad never stopped picking, but he tiptoed to the door and put one eye to the crack and got there in time to see Miz Grasshopper do the high jump. Rooster and Toad were so astonished, they couldn't speak; they just nudged one another with their elbows. Then Toad fell back on the bench and went on picking, and Rooster went and got up on the bench and crowed like he always did just before dinner.

When she heard him crow, Miz Grasshopper scampered back in bed and drew up the covers and pretended she couldn't move hand or foot. The Rooster walked in and came up toward the bed. "Well, ma'am, how are you this evening?" he asked.

She was panting so from the dancing that she scarcely could get her breath, so she rolled her eyes up in her head and said, "So poorly . . . I scarce . . . can talk."

"That's a burning fib!" cried Rooster. "I swear I'll make you get up from that bed and walk, Miz Pop-eyes!" Rooster snapped at one of her feet under the blankets.

She jumped out of the bed and raced for the door, and Rooster lit out after her with Toad cheering him on and playing runalong music lickety-split on his banjo. They certainly had a set-to then, for Grasshopper was a sure-enough jumper, and Rooster was a short-legged creature who looked like he would fall all over himself when he ran fast. They went tearing through the yard and over the fence and across a road and then back again, where Rooster almost chased Miz Grasshopper down the well. Then she made for the grass and thought she was going to hide away from him there, but he put on a big burst of speed and just about caught her. But he was so eager, he tripped on his own feet. This gave Miz Grasshopper just time enough to slip into the grass and escape.

Ever since then, roosters chase grasshoppers, because they can't forget Miz Grasshopper's deceitfulness. They won't leave a grasshopper alone when they see one but always try to run her down and gobble her up. And toads will dine on grasshoppers that come their way, too. So folks would have to say that Miz Grasshopper, by trying to get out of working, ended up getting herself into a mess of trouble. Put another way: creatures who think themselves too smart by half often find out they're only half as smart as they think they are.

Mistah Hare, Mistah Mink, and Miz Duck

O NE TIME MISTAH HARE MET UP WITH MISTAH MINK, who most folks thought was mighty clever. Hare put out his paw and shook hands and made himself most friendly. He pretended that he thought Mink was a mighty nice sort of fellow, but all the time he was searching around in his mind to find some way or other to show off and impress Mistah Mink with just how smart *he* was. Hare was never satisfied unless he let people know about his own cleverality. While he tried to think of a way to put himself forward, he said, "Mistah Mink, it's a mighty fine day; let's take a little walk together. Suppose we sashay around by the pond."

Mink said he would just as soon go that way as another, because the pond was one of his favorite spots; so they walked on and on until they finally reached the pond. There was a great big flock of ducks floating around in the water. Hare said, "They look so lazy it must be all the same come-day-go-day with them." But Mink told him, "Don't you be fooled: those ducks are scrabbling around for their food."

Hare watched them awhile longer, and then he said, "Mistah Mink, I don't want to show too much curiosity, sir, but just between friend and friend, I would like to ask you how you make your living? I see you looking right plump and pert for a man of your build, and I'd like to know the whys and the wherefores."

"Why, certainly," said the Mink. "I make my living right out in that pond without any trouble at all. When I want something to eat, I just jump right in and get a duck."

Hare started to wrinkle up his nose, kind of scornful; but he caught himself and said to Mink politely, "You don't say! Well, Mistah Mink, I would like to know just how you do that. Please, sir, show me how you catch a duck; I have been hearing all my days what a great hand you are at duck-catching."

That made Mink feel pretty good, so he said, "Well, then, just watch me closely, and I reckon maybe you'll be able to do it in the same manner."

Mink slipped into the water, dove under, then swam to where the ducks were floating, and they didn't even know he was near them. Then he caught one of them by the leg and pulled her under the water and dragged her over to where Mistah Hare was waiting.

"Uh-huh, Mistah Mink," Hare said, "very good. You did that mighty slick, sir. But I bet you I can do that same thing the very first time without the practice you've had all your days. The only thing needed here is to be handy and quick, sir—handy and quick." At this he twisted up the corner of his whiskers with one hand and looked mighty knowing.

"All right, sir," Mink said. "Dive in and let me see how you do. Maybe you can do it all right the first time, but I don't believe in any such shortcuts, myself. My experience is that you have to go around the long way if you want to do a thing well."

There was a log lying partway in the water near where the ducks were. Hare circled around to the place and waded out into the water and climbed up on the log, thinking he'd stand there and grab for a duck that way. But that time he misjudged. He nabbed for the nearest duck, but shoot! He lost his balance and fell into the water *ker-splash!* He came mighty close to drowning.

The ducks, who had been preoccupied searching for tasty frogs, heard the noise and hollered and quacked and flew off to the other side of the pond. One of the young ducks, who was just out for her first swim, said to one of the old ones, "*Quack, quack, quack!* Miz Duck, that was a great splash we heard. Must have been a mighty big frog that jumped into the pond."

"Umph," said the old lady. "Frog! I *say* frog! You've got to learn that frogs don't wear fur or you'll never have any peace or comfort in this pond. You don't know frogs yet when you see them, and you've got to make your living frog-hunting! I like that!"

"Well, ma'am," said the young one, "this is my first trip to the pond; you can't expect me to know everything you know, in a minute."

That sort of pleased Miz Duck, so she stopped scolding, and the others went on with their frog-hunting. But the older duck had gotten older because she kept her eyes and ears open and was always on the alert for mischief. She wanted to know what furry creature was splashing around on the other side of the pond and whether the commotion meant trouble for ducks. So over she paddled, keeping close to the brushy shore so whatever was splashing and spouting water wouldn't see her.

Meanwhile, Hare climbed up the bank more dead than alive, with his fur sticking to his hide and the water running off of him like rain. He was plenty aggravated, because hares don't like to get their feet wet—let alone their whole selves. He gave himself a shake and said, "Shucks! those are the triflingest ducks I've ever seen, frightened if someone shakes his little finger at them; and that old log was so slippery, you would have to have claws if you wanted to hold on to it."

"Never mind, Mistah Hare," said the Mink good-naturedly. "You must try your luck again. You mustn't give up on the first try. I'm gonna swim around to the other side of the ducks and drive the whole kaboodle back to this side. You must be ready to catch one, for I'm bound that you shall have duck for your dinner."

Of course, Hare wasn't going to let on that he was ready to give up the game so soon, so he blustered and said sort of carelessly, "Oh, well, if you say so, it isn't gonna faze me to catch one of them little no-count ducks. I've pretty much done what I set my mind to ever since I was knee-high to a grasshopper. I'm gonna nab one this time, you can be sure of that!"

So that's the game, is it! Miz Duck said to herself as she listened to water-logged Hare's boasting. *I think it might just do me good to settle the hash of that low-down, good-for-nothing creature!* In fact, Miz Duck had little use for Mistah Hare. He'd stolen more than one clutch of her eggs in the past, and she suspicioned that he knew more about the disappearance of Mistah Duck than he let on. She had heard how Hare and Mistah Slickry Sly-fox had been seen laughing together, thick as thieves, near the marsh where Mistah Duck had gone visiting kin. Duck had never reached his cousins. But folks said Fox seemed mighty well fed at the time, and Hare was heard telling how he slept better on a new duck-down pillow Molly Hare had sewn and stuffed for him.

"Well," Miz Duck said. "Let's just see who nabs who!" She swam back to the other side of the pond, where the young ducks were still frog-hunting. But she watched the far shore to see what would develop—and how she could turn things to her advantage and discombobulate old Hare.

Mink swam off, and Hare scrambled up on the bank and got himself a long piece of that brambly vine called the devil's shoestring. Well, he took the length of vine and crept down into the water with it until he was hidden, all but his nose and eyes. Soon, old Mink came splashing and yelling up a storm and driving the ducks toward the shore. As it turned out, old Miz Duck, the biggest and strongest of the lot, came sailing toward Mistah Hare. Hare was so excited to see such a fine duck falling into his trap he didn't pay attention to the hard way her eyes looked at him or the fact that she aimed herself straight as an arrow at the spot where his own eyes and nose bobbed just above the water. Miz Duck stopped a little ways from her sunken enemy.

38

Hare, thinking he had won the game, just grabbed her by the leg and held on while he tied her leg with the devil's shoestring. She made a great show as she quacked and she hollered and she flapped and she flew, making Hare think he had caught her by surprise. This made old Hare hang onto the brier even more tightly. "No use to kick, ma'am," he said, "'cause I got you this time, and I'm gonna hold on to you."

"Um-umph! I'm gonna show you how come," said the Duck with an angry little laugh, and she flew up and she flew up. Hare went spinning and wheeling and kicking, but he wouldn't let go—just as Miz Duck planned. Mink was standing down below, just a-hollering and a-laughing, clapping his hands on his knees and doubling himself up like a jackknife while all the young ducks paddled to safety. He sang out, "Hi-yi! Mistah Hare, you certainly have risen up in the world, sure enough. You have been right uppity before now; I don't reckon you're gonna speak with common folks after getting this high-and-mighty."

"I'll settle with you when I get back from this trip; I tell you that, point-blank," yelled old Hare, letting go with one hand long enough to shake his fist at Mistah Mink. Mink stood watching them and waving until Duck and Hare weren't anything but a speck in the sky. That Duck flew and she flew and she *flew*, and Hare held on until he thought his paws were going to drop off. He argued with her, and then begged her, "Please, ma'am, light somewhere and let me go." But she just quacked and said, "Can't hear you, sir; can't hear you. You have to speak louder, my ears aren't what they used to be."

When he couldn't hang on any longer, and he saw they were right over an old sycamore tree, he let go and dropped onto the tree. But the tree was hollow, so he just tumbled right down inside until he struck the ground. He was stunned at first, but after a while he sat up and looked around. It was mighty dark in there. He searched and he searched for some way to get out, but he didn't find any. He poked and he prodded and he tapped and he banged on the wood, but there he was, shut up tight with nothing but a little circle of daylight, way up at the top of the tree. From far overhead he heard Miz Duck calling, "Happy landings, you egg-thieving treacherous no-count! I hope you never get out."

As time passed, and Hare couldn't figure any way to break free, it seemed Miz Duck might get her wish. He got so hungry in his prison that he had to gnaw something, and since there wasn't anything else, he turned and nibbled his own tail off. That's why hares go around with short tails until this day.

At long last he heard someone chopping in the woods, and he said to himself, *Whatever the danger, I gotta attract the attention of that man if I want to get out.* "Hi-yi! Mistah Man," he called, speaking soft like a woman, "Oh, please, come here, Mistah Man."

Mistah Man couldn't hear him and went on with his chopping.

"Man must be deaf as a post," said Hare to himself. "I reckon I've gotta yell loud enough to bust my boiler if I want to get out of this." He tried it again, but the man still didn't hear. Then he thought maybe the man might hear him if he sang something, so he struck up an old tune and sang:

> *Oh! If I had a needle,*
> > *So fine that I could sew,*
> *I'd stitch my true love to my side*
> > *And down the river I'd go.*

He made his voice just like one of those high, fine ladies' voices that carry the sound a long ways, and at last Mistah Man heard him and he said, "Mercy me! What was that? It appears to me I hear a woman singing inside that tree."

He walked up and leaned his head against the tree to listen. Then he asked, "Are you all right, ma'am? I mean, you sure *sound* like a woman." At this Hare began to holler and cry and carry on to beat the band. He begged, "Oh, please, Mistah Man, take your ax and chop a hole in this tree and let me out. You told the truth; I *am* a woman, and a pretty one—at least folks tell me so—into the bargain. And if you let me out, I'm gonna give you a great big kiss for being my hero."

"All right," said the man, grinning to himself; because all men are more or less fools when it comes to the matter of a good-looking gal. So he chopped and he chopped, making the chips fly in his haste to get a sight of the gal that went with such a sweet voice. Hare had scrunched down in a corner out of the way of the ax. As soon as the hole was big enough, he took off like a rocket and went scooting out, right between the man's legs, into the brush. Just before he disappeared from sight, he laughed and yelled, "Hi-yi! Mistah Man, aren't I the fine shape of a gal? You can have a big old kiss if you can catch me!" And with that he was off, singing:

> Oh! If I had a needle,
> So fine that I could sew,
> I'd stitch my true love to my side
> And down the river I'd go.

That night Mistah Mink told Slickry Sly-fox, Otter, Bear, and Wildcat how Mistah Hare has "risen" in the world; their roars of laughter filled the woods. At the same time, Mistah Hare told Miz Hare and the children how he had fooled Mistah Man, and their laughter could be heard clear across the meadow. But none of this could match the laughter that floated above the pond where Miz Duck and the ducklings made merry over the way she had given what-for to "that trickish, egg-stealing, no-count Hare." And since this tale started up with mischief, but ended up in laughter, there wasn't much harm done (except to Hare's own tail, which ended up the shorter for it).

Miz Goose
Deceives Mistah Bear

PEOPLE SAY THAT GEESE ARE A KIND OF FOOLISH, SILLY sort of fowl; but, as Miz Goose once proved, they have a lot more sense than some of the folks that call them names. As for the ganders, there's not many a human man who takes care of his wife and family like a gander does of his. He helps the goose to build her nest, taking some of the down from his breast to help her line the nest, just as white and pretty as can be. While she sits on her eggs, he keeps guard. If any person comes near he beats his wings at them and does his best to drive them away. And when Miz Goose goes off to eat and rest herself, he just naturally squats down on the eggs and keeps them warm until she gets back.

When folks hear geese cry out in the night, that's because they are changing guard. For they sit a-watch all through the night and whenever they change, the watchman gives out a curious cry to say they are changing guard and everything is going on all right. No, geese aren't the weak-brains that folks have been calling them all these years. In fact, big and lumbersome as Mistah Bear is, there was a time when Miz Goose got the best of him.

She was waddling along one day with her children all strung out in a long line behind her. The goslings were very young, and she was taking them down to the stream to teach them to swim. She was mighty proud of them, and she was marching along with her head reared up, shooing them every now and then to keep them on the straight path, and cackling so that everybody could hear her.

"You, Fluff! You, Puff! You, Buff! You hear me? I want you all to keep on the path. Yonder is a dog; you better stick close to me if you know what's good for you!" So Fluff and Puff and Buff and all the rest of the little ones who had been looking to wander here and there turned their toes and went waddling along in a straight line down to the creek right behind their mama.

About that time they met up with Old Man Bear. He was staying out in the woods all by himself, and when he saw Miz Goose going along with all that nice family to keep her company, he got stricken with the notion that *he* wanted a family, too, to take around with him and cheer him up and drive away any low-down feelings. So he saluted Miz Goose mighty politely, touching his paw to his hat and saying, "Morning, Miz Goose; morning ma'am; I hope you are well."

She gave a little hiss and spread her wings and acted like she was going to run at him. She wasn't afraid of anybody, and she was mighty touchy when she looked after her children. Mistah Bear had never been very neighborly to Miz Goose and her kin, having made a meal of one or two of her cousins. But presently she saw that the creature wanted to be friendly with her, so she put her wings down and bobbed her head. "How are you doing yourself, Mistah Bear?" she said.

He allowed that he was feeling kind of blue, and that he felt the need of a family to keep him from getting lonesome. "When I saw you coming down the path with that nice, big family of yours, Miz Goose," he said, "I told myself, 'That's the care I've been needing for these-here low spirits of mine, though I didn't know what it was. I'm gonna ask her, this very minute,' I decided. And so I'm asking you, please ma'am, tell me how I can get myself a family like yours." Miz Goose leaned her head to one side and looked sharply up at him with one eye, the way geese do—because they never seem to look at you out of both eyes at once—and she saw he meant what he said; so she answered, "Well, sir, I hatched out these children from eggs."

"Is that so?" he said. "Well, ma'am, I'd be mighty obliged if you could tell me where I can get some eggs."

Right there Miz Goose was taken with a notion that made her laugh so hard on the inside that she could scarcely stand on one foot like she had been doing; she had to put both feet on the ground so that she could keep from shaking at all her bottled-up chuckling. But she didn't dare laugh out loud, and she never even smiled while she told him, "Heavens above! Mistah Bear, this is your lucky day! I know the very thing you need! Over yonder in the field is a whole nest full of eggs just waiting for someone to sit on them. I wish I'd been able to have undertaken that job myself, but you see my work is cut out for me already with these-here twelve little children of mine. I'm feeling poorly, too, from sitting so long on my own eggs. I've lost my spark, sir, done lost my spark, and my appetite isn't what it was. I'm gonna be honest with you, sir, and let you know that sitting is hard work, sir, that it is."

Bear said, "Bless your soul, Miz Goose, I'm not looking to get myself anything in this here suffering, dying world unless I work for it; and if a delicate lady like you can stand it, I reckon I can, big and strong as I am."

"Well, come on then, if you say so," Miz Goose said, and she led the way to a field where there was a pile of pumpkins in a fence corner. She pointed to these and said, "Here are the eggs, Mistah Bear. Now, sir, let me see you sit on them. You have got to cover every one of them with your body and keep them nice and warm, or else they aren't gonna hatch out and you'll have gone to all that trouble for nothing."

Bear never suspected that she was tricking him. He held to the view of most folks that geese were foolish creatures—too brainless to gull anyone. So old Bear squatted down on the pumpkins and he sprawled himself first this way and then that way, and drew his legs up and then put them down, and then got up and turned clean around and squatted again. Just when he thought he was all fixed up, here came a pumpkin rolling out first one side and then the other. Miz Goose was dying to laugh, but she didn't dare to, and at last she waddled over and helped to get him fixed up. Then she went off down the path with her family.

When she was far enough away, she began to chortle and chuckle so that the goslings began to wonder if their mama hadn't taken leave of her senses. She was still laughing so hard that she could barely speak when she met up with Miz Molly Cottontail. Miz Molly waited a little, and then she said, "You are a goose, for sure! Why don't you speak up like you had some sense and let me know the joke?"

Finally, Miz Goose told her about Mistah Bear and the eggs. Then Molly whooped and she hollered and held on to her sides. She didn't wait to say good-bye but just went hopping along the path until she came to the fence corner and saw old Bear. She didn't let on that she knew what he was up to; she just said, "Hey-o, Mistah Bear, what are you doing there, sir, lying in the fence corner this time of day?"

"Just resting myself, Miz Molly," he answered her, "just resting myself. I came a far ways and I'm trying to catch my breath again." Bear was afraid Molly would laugh at his family-raising effort.

She said, "This is a mighty fine day; I wish you would come for a walk with me."

But Bear just said he was too tired, and so Miz Molly said she would wait until he got rested. He begged her not to take so much trouble, and she said it wasn't any trouble at all, and they chatted on like that, powerful polite. All the time, though, Bear was feeling pestered and trying to think of how he was going to get rid of her. And he was afraid every minute that a pumpkin was going to roll out from beneath him.

All the time Molly Cottontail could scarcely keep her face straight, but at last she got tired of the fun and set out for home, telling him she would be back tomorrow to see if he was rested up.

Sure enough, bright and early next morning back she came to greet him. "Hey-o, Mistah Bear, I stopped by to tell you I found a tree up the road a mile or so, and it's so chock full of honey that it won't hold another drop. If you say so, I'll go right along with you and show you the way."

Bear licked his chops and acted like he was going to get up. Then he remembered the pumpkins and dropped back, and said, "Thank you, Miz Molly, thank you, ma'am. I'm feeling too sore-boned to go with you, I sure am, 'cause you know that I am plenty fond of honey."

Molly hung around, and Bear tried to get her to move along, but she told him she wasn't pressed for time, and that her old man and the children would keep until she got home. Every day she came back and asked him if he was well enough to go after the honey, and every day he said, "You must excuse me this morning, Miz Molly, you sure must; the spirits are honey-hungry, but the flesh is mighty weak, ma'am, mighty weak."

At last, she answered, "I believe you, sir; you certainly have grown weak and thin and spindle-shanked; you are nothing more than a shadow of the old Mistah Bear I knew."

Bear gave a groan, because he knew it was the truth. He hadn't been off the "nest" to get himself anything to eat because he was afraid the eggs might get cold, and so he was just about starved. He didn't dare to move, either, for fear the eggs might roll from underneath. He felt like he couldn't keep still another minute. Miz Molly Cottontail guessed that right well, but she kept on nagging and nagging at him until he growled to himself,

47

"Drat the woman," and then, "I wish I never thought about getting myself a family."

After more than a week of pumpkin-sitting, there came a day when Bear couldn't stand it any longer. He rose up and tried to stand, but he was so weak that he just fell back onto the pumpkins, and some of them rolled out from underneath and the rest were all squashed up, because they had commenced to get soft by that time. Bear groaned and he moaned and he cried and he rolled on the ground and dug both fists in his eyes. About then Miz Molly came along and heard the goings-on, and she stopped and hung over the fence pretending like she was mighty sorry. She said, "Mercy me, Mistah Bear, what do I see, sir? What is the occasion of all this misery?"

"Oh, dear! Oh, dear!" he moaned. "My poor family; my poor family!" and with that he busted out crying again. When he got so that he could talk, he said, "Miz Molly Cottontail, I ask you, ma'am, to look at these eggs I have been sitting on all this time, which I thought were gonna hatch out a nice little family. You see for yourself how most of them are all squashed up, and the rest have rolled away from me and gotten stone-cold. And here am I, hungry and thirsty and worn to the bone, all for nothing."

At that he cried louder than before. Then Miz Molly couldn't keep it in any longer. She leaned up against the fence and she yelled and she hollered. "Mercy! Mercy! If that don't beat all!" she cried, "He called them eggs, those big old rotten things are eggs! Well, live and learn, I say! Here I've been thinking all these years that those things were pumpkins, and now I find that they are eggs. If I had known what you were up to all this time, sir, I would have brought you some of that honey that I've been telling you about, 'cause you must be mighty hungry by this time. This here sitting business is mighty trying, I hear tell—so trying that the men most generally leave it to the ladies. Let me know next time you are gonna hatch out a family, and I'll try to help you get some vittles. You're a plumb skeleton; you sure are!"

Old Bear was getting kind of riled up by that time and acted like he was going to take after her. So she lit out from there lickety-split, but she saw he was too weak to follow her. She ran back for a minute and stuck her head through the fence and said, rolling one eye at the pumpkins and one at him, "Um-umph! Mistah Bear, this certainly is a pity, 'cause if them eggs had only hatched out, your family would surely have been *some pumpkins,* sure enough."

Then she scampered away before Bear could find the strength to light out after her. But she stopped to tell everyone she met the story of Miz Goose's joke. After that, no one in those parts ever used the words "as silly as a goose" again. Instead folks said a foolish person was "as silly as a bear hatching pumpkins."

Mistah Bear Tends Store for Mistah Fox

NOW MOLLY COTTONTAIL WAS MISTAH HARE'S WIFE, and she was as tricky as he was—sometimes more so—and that's saying a lot. She was a mighty smart female. She knew how to read and write; and, what's more, she could mimic the writing of most any person she wanted. This came near getting her into a heap of trouble once, but she was so slick, she wiggled out just in time. It fell out this way: Fox tried his hand at hunting and fishing and farming without making much of a go at any of them, and at last he set himself up a little general store at the crossroads—one of those stores where folks would bring in a little sack of vegetables from their garden or corn from their field and trade it for bacon and flour and such.

One day Miz Molly Cottontail had run out of something to eat, and her children were hungry and begging for food. She said to herself, "These children are gonna drive me to distraction. I have to stay home here and listen to all their botherment while their pa goes gallivanting around the country enjoying himself mightily. It isn't fair. But never mind, I've got to feed these children, and I know what I'm gonna do."

With that she sat down and took a piece of paper and an ink bottle and a quill pen, and she stuck the quill behind one ear and sat there thinking and running her fingers through the fur atop her head until she got a plan all fixed up in her mind. Then she took the quill and wrote an order to Mistah Fox at the general store nearby for a bag of cornmeal and some bacon and a few other things. Last off, she took it and signed Miz Fox's name to it, just exactly the way she had seen Miz Fox write her name one time. Then she sat down in the door and waited for some person to pass by.

First thing you know, here came Mistah Bear ambling down the road. By that time he had forgotten how Miz Molly had laughed at him about the pumpkins he tried to hatch like eggs, so when she greeted him, all nice and proper, he answered mighty politely. She didn't know how he was going to treat her, but when she saw it was all right, she commenced smooth-talking him, because she was a great hand at flattering folks. When she got things worked up to the proper pitch, she said, "Excuse me, Mistah Bear, I am essentially a shy woman and I hate to ask favors, but my children are hungry and there aren't any vittles in the house and their pa is away from home on business. I'd be mightily obliged, sir, if you would deliver this order for me at the crossroads store and bring me the vittles on your way back."

Bear said it wouldn't be any trouble. He took the order and left it at the store and then got the bacon and meal and what-not on the way back and fetched it along to Miz Molly. It wasn't long before it was all eaten up, and it wasn't much longer, either, before Mistah Fox found out the food he had given Bear was left with Miz Molly instead of with his wife. So he declared that he was going to get even with her for forging his wife's name.

Miz Hare didn't know Fox had found her out, so one day she went into the store to trade, biggity as you please. To her surprise, he asked her to keep store a minute while he stepped out. But he gave her such a sly look that she kind of smelled a rat, so she told him she didn't have time to tarry. But he grabbed her by the scruff of her neck, tied her up good and tight, and shouted,

"Uh-huh! Forge my old woman's name, will you? Eat up my meal and bacon, hey? Trash-of-the-world! I'm gonna go out and get my missus, and we're gonna give you the best thrashing you ever had or ever are gonna get."

He ran out and left her there studying the fix she was in. But while most persons would have felt more and more scared every minute, Molly wasn't fazed by it. Her brain-wheels were turning a mile a minute, and she was sure she'd figure a way out of her trouble pretty quick. She was so sure, she started humming one of these merry old dancing tunes and tapping with her feet, because her hands were tied behind her. At last she burst out at the top of her voice into the words of the song:

> Sam, Sam was a funny old man,
> Fried his meat in a frying pan,
> Combed his head with a wagon wheel,
> Died with the toothache in his heel.

About this time someone came sauntering down the road and heard the singing and poked his head in the door. Who should that be but Mistah Bear? He said, "Hey, Miz Molly Cottontail, what is the meaning of all this racket, and what are you doing all snarled up in that rope?"

"Well," she told him, spinning words as quick and trickish as Miz Spider spins her web, "I came here to get some calamine for my sick child, and Mistah Sly-fox told me he was gonna give a party at his house tonight, and he asked me to stay and join in the fun. But when I insisted I couldn't, 'cause I had to get back to my child, why he just swore that they couldn't get along without my company. They don't like to admit it, but those foxes are always hard up for friends. Then he told me he believed that I was too stuck-up to associate with his family, and had only made up that tale about the sickness of my child.

"I kept on telling him I couldn't stay, and finally I said I was going home. I took the calamine with me, and I started for the door. But he just said that a bird in the hand was worth two in the bush, so he took the rope and tied me up this-a-way so I'd have to stay until night. Then he stepped out to make ready for the party, and he asked me to mind the store while he was gone. Here I am, sitting here trying to keep my mind off my poor sick child by singing and keeping time with my foot. You haven't ever been a mother, Mistah Bear, or you would know just how I'm feeling this very minute." And right there she let two big tears fall down on the floor, *ker-splash!*

Bear felt mighty sorry when he saw that—men are so easily taken in by a few little old tears!—and he said that he would untie her, if she said the word, and let her go. She said, "Yes, sir. But Mistah Fox is gonna expect me to see that nothing got stolen out of the store; what am I gonna do about that? And they'll be expecting me at their party, so I guess you'll have to go in my place."

Bear said that he didn't mind tending the store a little, and she told him, "Go ahead, then, and untie me." When he had freed her, she said he had better let her tie him up in the same place so that he couldn't change his mind about staying for the party. Bear said he wasn't hankering after any festivities, but if there was any food to be eaten at the party, he was the fellow for the feast. When Molly assured him that there'd be vittles enough to stuff himself ten times over, he let her tie him up. Then she went clipping down the road, stopping at the turn long enough to sing out, "Oh, Mistah Bear! Oh, Mistah Bear! I hope you enjoy yourself at the party! They tell me it's gonna be mighty small and select. It wouldn't surprise me if you had to do most of the dancing yourself as well as most of the eating, naturally!" With that she went scooting off—but after a bit, she slipped into the brush and doubled back and hid by the store to watch and listen.

Presently Mistah Fox came loping back, holding Miz Fox by the hand.

They were more than surprised when they saw old Bear tied fast in the place where Fox had left Miz Molly Cottontail. "Mercy me!" Fox bellowed. "What in the name of the ring-tail-roarers is the meaning of this here piece of business? Who tied you up this-a-way?"

"It was that Molly Hare, I'll be bound!" said Miz Fox.

"The same," Bear confessed. "And I'm the one's been bound."

"How did that happen?" Fox asked.

"Well, sir," Mistah Bear answered, "she told me you tied her up to make her stay for your party tonight, and she said she was only pining to get home to her sick young one. She cried a little and begged a little, and finally I told her I would just as soon take her place and tend the store and go to the party."

Fox curled his mustache and twisted the ends up and looked at old Bear out of the corner of his eye and said: "Uh-huh, is that so? You told her that, did you? You were willing to stay for the party? Well, if that's the case, can you tell me why she had to go to work and do you up in all those hard knots?"

Bear said, "That's all right. I turned her loose, and then she tied me up this way 'cause she was afraid I might change my mind about staying for the party. So she said she had best make sure of me, since you foxes were so hard up for friends that you had to do things this way to get anybody to come to your gathering."

That made Miz Fox madder than a nest of hornets, but Mistah Fox found he wasn't too mad to laugh and holler and slap his hand on his knee. "My, oh my!" he cried. "If that Molly isn't one smart female! Well, sir, the only party me and Miz Fox were gonna give was a thrashing party, and Miz Hare was the only folks invited. Now, sir, since you let the chief guest go, you're gonna be the guest in her place, and take the presents we was gonna give her." Then Mistah Fox hit Mistah Bear with a sack of cornmeal and Miz Fox pelted him with cabbages and eggs.

Bear reared and he thumped and he tore and he swore and he growled and he howled, but it wasn't any use: Miz Molly had tied him up good and fast.

"I'm gonna teach you some sense, you great big pumpkin-hatching galoot!" cried Mistah Fox. "I'm gonna teach you not to be taken by every little old female who can pump the water out of her eyes in three shakes of a sheep's tail!"

"I'm gonna teach you not to meddle in other folks' affairs," yelled Miz Fox.

Finally Mistah Fox said, as he emptied a jar of molasses over Bear, "You are the very creature who came here and brought me that order from my missus which never came from her at all; and it was you that toted off the meal and bacon to old Molly Cottontail. Don't you know that female well enough by now to know that you'll get in trouble if you don't keep away from her?"

"Indeed!" added Miz Fox. "You are old enough to know better, indeed you are; anyhow, I'm gonna teach you." And with that, she burst an old feather pillow across Mistah Bear's chest, so the goose down stuck every-which-way to the molasses.

All this time, old Bear was crying one big "*Boo-hoo!*" after another. Miz Molly was sitting outside listening, and every time he said, "Boo-hoo!" she laughed, "Ho-ho!" at the same moment, so they didn't hear her at all. After this, the foxes turned Mistah Bear loose.

Molly popped out of the brush and said, "Why, is that you, Sis' Goose? Your feathers seem ruffled, they do indeed!" Mistah Bear roared and grabbed for her, but she bounded away in a jiffy, and Bear didn't see her for a long spell after that. He had to stay home and clean off the molasses and fluff for a while, and he vowed to goodness that he was going to fix Molly right and proper the next time he met up with her. "Miserable little five-penny-bit," he snarled. "For her to get a great big fellow like me a thrashing from that old Slickry Sly-fox and his missus! I'll knock them all into the middle of next week next time I catch 'em, dog me if I don't."

Finally, one day, Molly saw him coming down the road, and she turned off into the brush and scooted through a shortcut until she got way beyond him. Then she hopped into the middle of the road and sang out, "Hey-o, Mistah Bear, how did you enjoy yourself at the foxes' party? I told everyone that you were the favoritest guest at the doings, and that you were dressed so special, no one—male or female—ever wore the like." With that, she gave her back legs a flick in the air and went plunging into the brush again, like the devil himself was after her, which maybe he was, considering all her mischief.

Miz Molly Cottontail might have had an easier time of things if she hadn't been so quick with a trick every time the chance came along. Or if she hadn't gone and rubbed salt into the wounds of folks she got the better of. But more than anything, Molly loved to laugh. And the best part of the jokes she pulled was letting folks know she was laughing at them. What she did might rile folks up for a time; still, they'd probably forget and maybe even forgive in a little more time. But Molly would always be there, chuckling and reminding them how she'd made them play the fool. That's why so many folks carried a grudge against her—and were always looking for ways to outwit her. She was just lucky her brain could hatch ideas for getting her out of hot water as fast as it hatched mischief that got her there in the first place.

Mistah Fox
and Sis' Duck

S IS' DUCK WAS A LITTLE RUNT OF A FOWL, BUT SHE HAD
plenty of sense. One time she fooled Mistah Fox, sure enough. That was
nothing to sneeze at, because Fox is mighty smart and up to snuff and
can dodge the hounds and the hunters, as clever as you've seen. But Sis' Duck
knew how to bamboozle him somehow or other.

One time she went waddling down to the creek, talking away to herself hard
as she could, running on quacking and scolding about this and that. Mistah Fox
was nosing around through the woods when he heard her, and he said to himself, "Here's where I'm gonna get me a good meal; I reckon she's just about big
enough to fill me chock-full, and she looks right young, so I expect she's plenty
plump and tender." He smacked his lips and went racing ahead and squatted
down behind a tree beside the path Sis' Duck was following. And when she got
near to him, he jumped out and nabbed her by the neck and flung her across his
shoulder. Holding her by her webbed feet, he went along singing:

> *Chick-a-lee? Chick-a-lee?*
> *Are you a friend to me?*
> *If you aren't you oughtta be!*
> *Chick-a-lee? Chick-a-lee-lee?*
> *Chick-a-lee?*

All the time he was singing, Sis' Duck was hanging head down, just twisting and scuffling, but it wasn't any use: Fox held on, he did, and he just let her go on jawing all she wanted. After a time she stopped her racket and set her mind to work on the question of how to get out of the pickle she was in. Presently she said, "Excuse me, please, sir, Mistah Slickry Sly-fox, I'd like to talk to you a little bit, but it's mighty hard work with my head hanging down so. I ask you, please lift my head a little higher, sir."

"Now, ma'am," Fox said, "I know enough to hold on to a good thing when I get it."

"Mercy me, Mistah Fox," Sis' Duck replied. "You are mighty flattersome in your remarks. I'm not gonna try to cheat you out of your dinner, indeed I'm not. But while we're jogging along here, I'd just like to ask you, sir, if you like to eat pig?"

"Now you're talking," said Fox, and he smacked his lips so loud that it sent cold shivers up and down Sis' Duck's spine. "What's the matter, Sis' Duck?" he said. "What are you shivering about this warm day?"

She was too proud to let on that she was scared, so she said, "Oh, nothing at all, Mistah Fox, just a little touch of the ague; you know when you got that you're obliged to shiver, never mind how warm the day is." Then she went on saying, "So you sure enough like pig, sir. I heard tell that you did, but I wasn't sure about it."

Her talk had got Fox's mind on pig, and now it seemed like he couldn't get it off thoughts of ham and bacon and chops. Finally he got kind of mad because there wasn't any pig to be had, and he said, "Look here, woman, I don't know why you mentioned that meat to me when you know I can't get any."

Sis' Duck said, "Now, I ask you to tell me the plain truth, sir: which do you prefer, pig or duck?"

Fox replied, "Give me pig every time, 'cause it doesn't have any feathers. I tell you, ma'am, when you swallow duck down the way I do, feathers and all, your throat gets mighty woolly for a fact. I sometimes think I'll choke to death on duck one of these days."

Serves you right, and I hope you will, Sis' Duck thought to herself. Then she sang out, "So you prefer pig, sir! Put me down, then, land knows! I'll show you where you can get yourself a whole litter of pigs!"

Fox said, "Well, ma'am, you lead me to those pigs, and mind you walk straight, for if I find any fooling about this business, I'm not gonna give you time to say your prayers. You just mosey 'long in front of me, please, ma'am."

She led him round and round to a place where a hillock rose sharply out of the ground, and she pointed it out to him. Then she told him, "Behind there is a juicy litter of pigs. But to catch them, you must run from a ways off and jump off the hillock right into the middle of the pigs. That way you'll surprise them, so that you can get them easily."

Old Fox agreed to this, so he ran back a little ways, took a big breath and spit on his hands, threw one foot in front and the other one behind, and teetered back and forth a minute to get a good swing on. Then he burst into a run, raced up the steep side of the hillock, crested it, then leaped into the air, landing like a lighting hawk in the midst of the litter. But it wasn't any litter of pigs; it was old Miz Dog and her pups.

"Ow! wow!" she yelped. "Who is this audacious creature that comes raring and charging into my house, disturbing me and my family? If it isn't that good-for-nothing piece of impudence, Old Man Fox! I'm gonna show you what for, that I will! I'll let you know that you can't come destroying the peace of respectable folks any such way as that. Stay here one minute longer, and I'm gonna put my paw down your throat!"

With that, Fox leaped out of the place a heck of a lot faster than he got in and just went scooting away, Miz Dog after him, hot-foot, snapping at his hindquarters. Sis' Duck was behind the hillock just snickering and snorting. Fox caught sight of her, and he shook his paw and cried out, "Never mind, Sis'

Duck, you are the occasion of all this rumpus. I reckon you think this here is a mighty funny prank you played on me, but I'm gonna pay you back for this; just you wait, ma'am. You're gonna take another free ride on my shoulder before you know it, and that time you won't get off so easy. You can pin it down in your memory that I'm gonna pay you back with interest on the money."

Sis' Duck knew he didn't dare to stop right then, so she let out one big hoot and teased him, saying, "Do so, Mistah Fox, do so. Now is your time, sir; the sooner the better. Why don't you stop, sir? You aren't ever gonna catch me any younger. Better not wait, sir; the longer you wait, the older and tougher I grow."

But Old Man Fox knew too much to stop when Miz Dog was at his heels, so he went tearing off and left Sis' Duck standing by the puppies just quacking and cackling and laughing fit to beat the band. What happened to Mistah Fox made him plenty mad; but what made him angrier was the song Sis' Duck made up and sang to anyone willing to listen:

> *Old Fox jumped clean over the hill,*
> *when Sis' Duck told him do it.*
> *He hoped to get a bit of pig,*
> *but he's the one got bit.*

Old Man Fox made up his mind to get revenge on the duck. "And this time there won't be no chitchat, neither," he promised himself. "Pounce and swallow, that's my plan." So he took to lurking beside the path from Sis' Duck's house to the Big Pond, where she would visit every day with her sisters and cousins and aunts. But the duck spotted him and refused to leave her house. She hoped he would soon grow tired of waiting, and leave her be; but Fox was set on getting revenge—and he knew a duck just naturally needs to go to water and gossip with her female kin every so often. So he lurked and lurked some more.

Soon enough, the lack of pond and palaver took its toll. Sis' Duck took to pacing back and forth in her house. But every time she opened her front door and looked up the path to the pond, she would see Fox's snout or tail peeking out from the brush. Then she would slam the door and go on with her pacing.

One day she was sitting on the back stoop, feeling mighty depressed, and studying how she could get to the pond without getting pounced on and eaten by Fox. Presently, she spotted Poor Miz Skunk. Sis' Duck had always been sociable to her, because the sad creature had few friends—and she always looked a mess in her raggedy clothes.

"Hey-o, Miz Skunk," the duck called. "I wonder if you could do me a kindness? I been feeling poorly—it's my delicate stomach. And I know my family at the Big Pond must be worried. Will you go along and tell them I'm on the mend, indeed I am. If you do this, I'll let you wear my Sunday-to-meetin' dress and gloves and hat with the veil, yes, ma'am!"

Skunk might have done this out of feeling neighborly; but the chance to wear Sis' Duck's fancy clothes clinched things. She kept spinning and spinning around to see herself in the mirror as the duck dressed her in a gown whose billowy skirts concealed her bushy black-and-white tail; in a long, lovely shawl that hid her claws; and in a veil that covered her furry face.

Down the path to the Big Pond she headed; but Poor Miz Skunk had only gone a few steps, when Fox—seeing her in Sis' Duck's finery and thinking it was the duck in fact—pounced.

"Rapscallion! Highwayman! Good-for-nothin'!" screeched the skunk. "I'll show you how come!"

And she did what a skunk does best.

Fox scurried away, but he could not escape. The skunking lingered for weeks, so Miz Fox made him eat and sleep on the porch. After this, Mistah Fox decided to leave Sis' Duck alone. And ever since that time there hasn't been much love lost between the foxes and the ducks. But then, there hadn't been much before, either.

The Foxes and
the Hot Potatoes

ONE WINTER NIGHT OLD JACK FROST WAS AT HIS WORST—whooping and hollering around the house, whistling through the keyholes, rattling the windows, and reaching up through the cracks in the floor to pinch folks by the toes. Old Man Hare and Miz Hare and the children were all scrunched up by the fire trying to keep warm, waiting and watching for the potatoes that were roasting in the ashes.

"Mercy on me!" said Mistah Hare, hitching himself closer to the hearth. "There isn't anything in this living world that's gonna take me out of the house tonight. I'm gonna stay right here along with you-all and toast my shins and smoke my pipe. It's cold enough outside to freeze the horns off a buffalo. Old woman, get out the teakettle and let's have a little tea all around to warm us up, and by that time the potatoes will be good and done."

So Miz Hare served them all around with tea, and then she commenced to pull out the potatoes, while the children sat up on their haunches watching her with their big, bright eyes, working their noses and smacking their chops like they could scarcely wait. That must have been a sight, Miz Molly scratching away in the ashes with her little old white cottontail turned up in the air and her back feet just a-flying.

While she was working, the children were grabbing the potatoes, and the old man had to do a little cuffing and scolding. He said, "You, Jumper and Thumper! I want you to stop snatching from Bunny and Honey; they're the babies, and they can't look out for themselves. You oughtta be ashamed of yourselves! Winker and Blinker, you needn't think I don't know that you're sneaking potatoes and hiding them behind your backs. Put them back and go share all around, or I'll come over there and cuff you good, so help me bob!"

As Miz Hare went on drawing out the hot potatoes, she got mighty warm. At last her paws began to smart, and she said, "Land of the living! This here is too hot for me; let me get out to where I can cool my paws. Never mind if I get the chilblains; I might as well freeze as burn up."

With that she made for the door, and when she opened it, there stood Mistah Fox, just shivering and shaking with the cold. He was trying to think of some way to do the Hares out of their dinner, but his brain was too cold to work properly. Miz Molly knew right away he was up to some mischief, so she said, "Hey-o! Mistah Fox; this here's a nice warm evening you've selected for your visit. Will you have a chair just outside the door?"

With his teeth just clattering and chattering, Fox said, "Please, ma'am, Miz Molly Cottontail, let me come in this very minute and don't stand there yakking with me, 'cause I'm frozen to the marrow and I'm obliged to get thawed out or else drop right here in my tracks."

"Well," Molly said, "I don't know about letting you in; this is a mighty cold night, and we've got just a tiny fire and a lot of paws to be warmed at it, for you know I've got some eleven or more children in my family." Then she stroked her chin thoughtfully. "But I reckon I might make out to let you in if you'll undertake the job of digging a lot of potatoes out of the ashes."

"Let me get in," said the Fox. "I'm good for all night at that job. Just let me get my feet in those ashes once and I won't take them out in a hurry."

"Well, then," she said, "walk in and make yourself at home; we're gonna give you a mighty warm welcome." And right there she grinned behind Fox's back and winked at Old Man Hare. "Get your mouths ready, now, children!" she sang out to the young ones.

Old Fox just started scratching in the ashes like he was possessed, and the children sat there and gobbled potatoes faster than he could dig them out. Finally he began to get kind of hot, and he cried, "Ouch! Ouch! Ouch!"

Miz Hare said, "What's the matter, Mistah Fox, aren't your feet warm yet?"

Fox didn't say anything; he just went on a-scratching, but presently his paws were so scorched and singed that he couldn't stand it. "Jiminy Cricket!" he cried. "Miz Hare, you must let me out of this job, you surely must. I reckon the children have got their fill by this time, anyhow."

"No we haven't, Mammy! Make him go on," the young ones yelled, and Miz Hare said, "You heard that now. I can't let my children go hungry, so I'm obliged to ask you to go on, or else me and my old man gotta fling you out in the cold."

Fox sat and thought a minute about which was the worse, the fire or the frost, and finally he made up his mind to try the fire a little longer. He was also hoping to get a potato for himself before they were all gone. So he went on with the scrabbling for a while, but finally he couldn't stand it any longer, and he burst out yelling, "Ow! Ow! Ow! *Ouch!* Let me out of this! Put me in the cold or any place where I can cool my feet! *M-m-m-m-umph!* Feels like my feet are burnt clean off of me!"

With that, he ran out and buried his paws in the snow, while the Hares slammed the door behind him. After this, Fox went limping along a little ways, colder than ever, just thinking how he was going to get back by that fire. Presently, he met up with another fox, a little young fellow, easy to fool, and he said to him, "Hey-o, young fellow, what are you doing cantering around on this cold night; does your mammy know you're out? You had better come along and go back with me to Old Man Hare's. They have a rip-roaring fire there and a lot of potatoes roasting, and they'll let you get warm and give you a potato, too, just for pulling them out of the ashes."

Mistah Young-fox said, "Well, Mistah Slickry Sly, I don't mind if I do." So they went along back to old Hare's house and knocked, and Slickry explained that he had brought somebody to pull potatoes out of the ashes. So Miz Hare invited them in and set the young fellow to work.

He was mighty quick about it at first, but it wasn't long before he slacked up, and presently he was grunting and groaning and licking his paws. Old Fox sat there and egged him on and ate potatoes with the family and hollered and laughed when at last Young-fox dropped a hot potato and bolted for the door. "Don't be in such a hurry," Slickry called out after him. "You're gonna find mighty cold weather outside."

Miz Hare put on a solemn look and said, "Mistah Slickry Sly-fox, aren't you ashamed to make fun of your fellow creature?"

Fox responded, "Naw, that I'm not. You've heard before now that misery loves company. And someone else's misery can be mighty funny!"

Old Man Hare let on like he was put out with such talk, and he just took his foot and gave Fox a boot that landed him outside the door, which Molly had pulled open. Hare said, "Take that, now, and run along, and don't you come here anymore talking any such way as that in front of my little children; I don't want them to learn such behavior to their fellow creatures. You hear me, sir! Now mosey 'long, before I give you what-for again. I don't want to hurt you, indeed I don't."

Then Molly shut the door and came back, and Mistah Hare cuffed the children all around for scrabbling in the ashes and getting themselves dirty; and then they all went to bed and slept soundly, ignoring Jack Frost, who continued to whistle through the keyholes and rattle the doors all the cold night through.

While Molly slept, her nose twitched and her mouth turned up in a grin, as she relived in her dreams all the tricks she had played on Mistah Fox and others. And new ideas were coming to her about jokes she could play in the future. And if she wasn't sleeping the high-toned sleep of the just, at least she was enjoying the low-down sleep of the jester. Meanwhile, Mistah Slickry Sly-fox had found himself a snug little den. At first, he had a hard time falling asleep, because of the aches and pains of his burned paws and kicked hindquarters. But when he finally did nod off, he enjoyed dreams in which he settled past scores by fooling Miz Molly Cottontail over and over.

Sleeping or waking, Molly and Slickry were just naturally of a trickish turn of mind. And if their doings didn't make the world a finer place, at least they kept it livelier and filled with laughter.

SISTER TRICKSTERS

Rollicking Tales of Clever Females